Silent Samurai and the
Magnificent Rescue

By Eileen Wacker • Illustrated by Alan M. Low

ISBN 978-1-938806-01-8

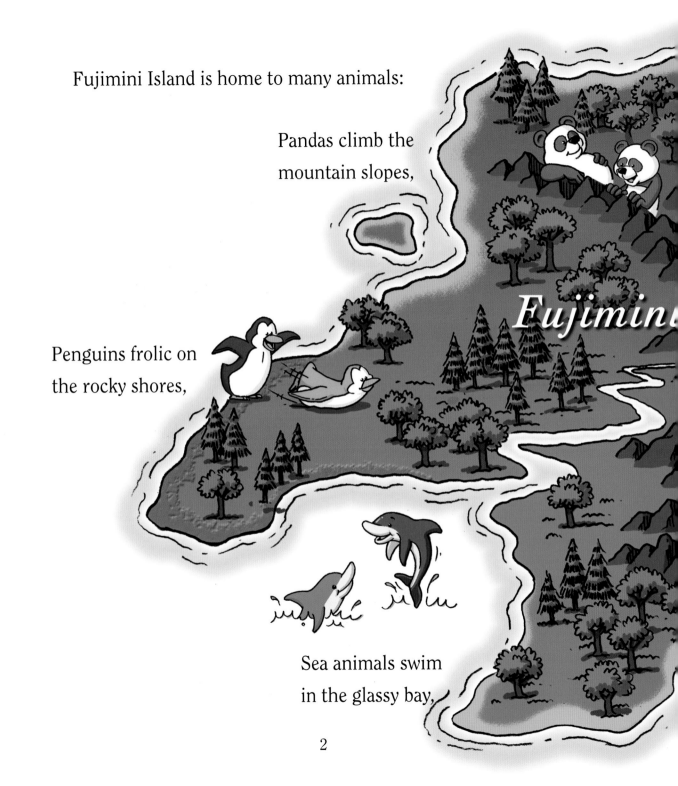

Fujimini Island is home to many animals:

Pandas climb the
mountain slopes,

Penguins frolic on
the rocky shores,

Sea animals swim
in the glassy bay,

2

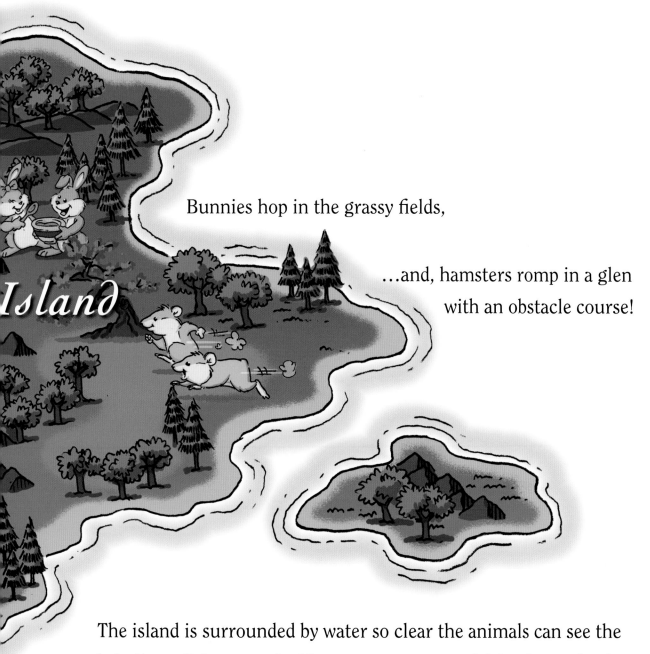

Bunnies hop in the grassy fields,

...and, hamsters romp in a glen with an obstacle course!

Island

The island is surrounded by water so clear the animals can see the sandy bottom. It is covered with evergreen trees so high, they poke the clouds. Each day, many animals gather under a beautiful bonsai tree.

3

Today, Purple Penguin hurries over to the bonsai tree, waiting for the others to arrive. He is flapping his flippers and making a commotion. He keeps squawking, "I have big news. I have really big news!"

Brown Hamster, Black Panda and Blue Bunny go to the bonsai tree to hear the news. Purple Penguin says, "Finally, you are here! I just heard from Blue Bay Dolphin that Samurai and a raft carrying their equipment are approaching Fujimini Island! They must be on a special mission. Isn't this exciting? It's like royalty coming to visit! Please go back and tell everyone we must plan an amazing welcome party."

Purple Penguin is so excited he doesn't notice that the others are not happy. They are quietly concerned that the Samurai may have come for a battle.

Brown Hamster goes back to the glen and reports to the other hamsters. "Purple Penguin says that Samurai warriors are coming for some special, secret mission."

Green Hamster immediately thinks about holding one of their shiny swords.

Pink Hamster suggests a party with cake.

Brown Hamster quietly wonders if they should prepare for a party or a sword fight.

"I think we should stay here and let the others greet the Samurai until we know what their mission is," says Brown Hamster. "There could be trouble. They are warriors after all."

"If there is trouble, we can always run away," offers Blue Hamster. "Since we run Hamster Races every day, we are very fast." Brown Hamster responds, "Yes, but we just run in circles so it might be easy to catch us!"

Green Hamster whispers, "I just have to hold one of those shiny swords. We're going!"

Over in the grassy field, the bunnies are also worried about the arrival of the warriors. "Why are they coming?" they ask. "Let everyone else meet them first." Orange Bunny, the island's *taekwondo* instructor says, "We are taught to fight only when there is no other option. But just in case, we should practice our *taekwondo* exercises all morning." Later, they plan to hop to hiding places and watch the visitors' arrival.

The pandas also discuss the news of the visitors. Brown Panda says, "I heard Samurai are good hiders. They may try to take our best trees to set up an attack." Black Panda agrees, "I am not sure I want them to come. Let's stay up on the mountain and watch."

Yellow Panda runs into the woods throwing firecrackers, shouting, "I'm going to scare away the bad luck. Bang Bang! Go away bad luck!" Orange Panda starts making giant bowls of noodles saying, "With warriors coming, we'll need long noodles for a long life!"

Purple Penguin is confused as he watches the animals prepare for the Samurai arrival and says to Red Penguin, "What a commotion. We should be preparing gifts and a special welcome party. This is not honorable. The Samurai will think we are impolite."

Red Penguin nods her agreement but all of a sudden she hears Blue Bay Dolphin in the distance making loud clacking noises. "Something must be wrong. Let's ask Blue Whale to go out and investigate."

They call out to the reclusive Blue Whale who swims over excitedly. He is so happy to be included that he is flapping his big flippers up and down. "Blue Whale, please calm down! You are splashing everyone."

"Sorry, I can do this. I want to help!" exclaims the Blue Whale. "Give me a chance. I won't even stop for a snack." He sets off to find out why the Blue Bay Dolphin is making clacking noises.

Shortly after, Blue Whale returns and reports, "The boat carrying the Tortoise Samurai's equipment is sinking after being hit by a storm. They are swimming next to the boat, trying to hold it up. But they can't keep it floating much longer."

Purple Penguin starts panicking. He is hopping, flapping and squawking, "Aaaacckk! Aaaacckk! The Samurai are in trouble!"

Other animals come over to see what all the fuss is about and hear the news about the sinking equipment.

The animals start talking all at once. "Surely the tortoises know how to swim?" exclaims Orange Bunny. "Is their equipment too heavy? Will their swords sink like stones?" Green Hamster asks. Purple Penguin just says, "Oh dear! I don't know. Tortoises can swim, but they must need their equipment for the special mission."

Black Panda takes charge and says, "Okay everyone, we need to do something." Suddenly the animals run, scamper and hop toward the penguin coast. They decide to work together to strengthen a raft to rescue the Samurai's equipment. Then the tortoises can safely swim to shore on their own.

The pandas are very strong and gather giant branches. "Hamsters," they cry, "Use your paws to twist vines into rope and bind the branches!" The hamsters run and bind in unison. The raft is getting stronger.

The bunnies use their *taekwondo* moves to break branches quickly as Orange Bunny shouts, *"Hana, tul, set!"* Everyone is impressed and Green Hamster secretly vows to practice his *taekwondo* kicks more.

They quickly finish the raft. The penguins, who are at the water's edge, call out to Blue Whale, "Pull the raft to the Samurai! Then tow the equipment to shore."

The Samurai silently stare at the animals as they approach. The animals jump to the broken boat and start moving the equipment.

Blue Bay Dolphin is clicking, "Hurry! Save the equipment before it sinks!"

The quiet Tortoise Samurai don't say anything. They just swim along silently next to the raft and the animals.

When they reach the shore, the animals gather to get a closer look at Black Tortoise Samurai. His face is a little fierce but also friendly and kind. His eyes twinkle with mischief, making him appear fun.

"Wow, they are not scary after all, but they sure don't talk a lot," whispers Green Hamster, "And, look at those swords!"

Black Tortoise Samurai clears his throat. "We were sent on a special mission to solve the mystery of the Dynasty Dragon. We would have lost our equipment without your magnificent rescue."

Green Hamster asks, "Quiet Mr. Warrior, is part of your mission to attack us? Have you come for a sword fight?" The other animals hold their breath, surprised that Green Hamster asked, but wondering the same thing.

"Oh, my goodness," replies Black Tortoise Samurai, "we are not here to fight anyone! We are only here to search for something very special for the Emperor."

All the animals start dancing and cheering. Blue Bunny shouts, "Let's have a party under the bonsai tree to welcome our new friends." Everyone agrees that would be fun.

The pandas rush to get the long noodles and firecrackers for the celebration. The bunnies offer to have a *taekwondo* show for the Samurai and bring a cake. Purple Penguin is very proud and makes an announcement. "Honorable Samurai, we are humbled by your visit. Please accept our simple feast and performance as a sign of our friendship."

Black Tortoise Samurai lets Green Hamster touch the shiny sword. "Maybe you will grow up to be a warrior someday," he says. "Today you were all warriors. Thank you for your kindness and open welcome. Tomorrow we shall discuss how to repay your kindness." The Samurai bow to the animals.

Brown Hamster says, "It was wise to welcome new friends even if they are Samurai warriors. We worked well as a team and great things happened. It is one of the best days on Fujimini Island! Let's rest up. Who knows, the Samurai may need our help solving the mystery of the Dynasty Dragon."

Everyone laughs and waves goodnight to their new friends, ready to sleep.
And, Green and Pink Hamster bow to the friendly Black Tortoise Samurai and
skip back to the glen. Along the way, they make a secret pact to join the special
mission.

FUJIMINI
ISLAND

Glossary of "Chic"
Asian Associations

At ONCEKids, we love and feel inspired by Asian cultures. So there are lots of references in the Fujimini Adventure Series about special aspects of Korean, Chinese and Japanese culture.

Here's a glossary to help explain some of the elements in the stories you may not be familiar with. Did you know about any of the cultural items before? Did you pick them up in the stories? After reading this, you may want to go back and read some of the stories again!

Bonsai Tree means "tree in a tray" if you translate directly into English. But a bonsai tree is actually so much more. The art of the bonsai tree is really telling a story and capturing the spirit of beautiful, living things and has roots in Zen Buddhism. The bonsai art started in China and spread to Korea and Japan. The Japanese are very famous for their beautiful and graceful bonsai creations. Although they are miniature in real life, on Fujimini Island, the bonsai tree represents the special meeting place of the animals and is a full size tree they gather underneath.

Chopsticks are very popular and widely used across Asia. In many Asian cultures, people eat with chopsticks (and sometimes a spoon) instead of a knife and fork. Since knives and forks are made from steel, they are sometimes thought of as more rough and sharp than the chopsticks. In fact, it is said that Confuscius taught: "the honorable and upright man allows no knives at his table." Some people are superstitious about chopsticks — for example, some believe uneven chopsticks may lead to a missed event and dropped chopsticks can be bad luck.

Dim Sum means "touch the heart" in Cantonese and was originally meant to be just a snack. Dim sum comes in many forms like dumplings, buns, steamed rice, spring rolls, and sweets. Older people enjoy these delicious dumplings after their morning exercises while in the afternoon, hardworking workers stop into teahouses hungry for dim sum. People around the world eat dim sum around the clock. But Black Panda warns, "Careful! Too much dim sum and you'll look like a round dumpling yourself!" The pandas are the best dim sum makers on the island and make all sorts of dumplings, sticky buns and steamed and spring rolls.

Dragons in Asia are not mean and scary dragons, but they are POWERFUL! They are considered fair and can bring wealth and good fortune. They are also one of the four protectors in Asian culture. The dragon can be a "shape shifter" which means it can change its form. Sometimes it is believed that the dragon's breath can change into clouds that can become rain or fire. There will be a mystery involving a white baby dragon coming to the Fujimini Adventure Series so keep watching!

Lighting **Firecrackers** is a popular form of fun on many holidays. The Chinese invented the first firecrackers! For a thousand years, setting off fireworks was used to keep away bad things, get rid of evil, or use against invading armies. Now, it is much more common to light these off for holiday celebrations, especially New Year's! Yellow Panda really loves fireworks — so much so that Black Panda keeps them hidden away except for special occasions. Yellow Panda also believes in lighting fireworks to keep away bad luck.

In China, **Lanterns** symbolizes joyfulness. The happiest days are filled with lanterns. Some examples of happy days are weddings, Lunar New Year and the end of moon festival celebrations. Lanterns are a symbol of enlightenment and blessing. The earliest lanterns were hung as a means of communicating a birth, a death, social status and danger. Today they are more aesthetic. Red lanterns are present at every major Chinese festival and represent people's happiness and joy. Chinese people around the globe hang lanterns where they live – watch for them during the coming Chinese (lunar) New Year!

In the Chinese culture, **Long Noodles** represent a long, healthy life. They are an important part of New Year and birthday celebrations. Orange Panda is the noodle maker on Fujimini Island and makes sure to make long noodles for their important parties. She also makes GIANT bowls of noodles if she senses trouble may be coming as she wants to ensure they eat long noodles for long lives!

The round **Moon Cake** looks like a full moon in the clear night sky. For more than a thousand years, families throughout China, Korea and Japan have gathered in the fall for moon harvest celebrations. This is a wonderful tradition. Families get together, eat moon cakes, sing moon songs and recite romantic poetry about the moon. Even if a family member is away, they look up at the sky and feel happy knowing they are looking at the same moon. The moon cake is a Chinese symbol of reunion.

The Moon Festival is one of the most important traditions for the Chinese (and now Koreans and Japanese as well!). It is normally celebrated as a mid-autumn festival. It is a great time for people to spend time with family and if they cannot, they can take comfort in knowing that they are gazing at the same moon as their loved one. This gives a feeling of optimism and happiness.

Peaches originated in China in the 10th century BC and were the favored fruit of Emperors. In China, Japan, Korea, Laos and Vietnam, peaches are very popular and many myths are associated with it. For example, Momotaro, one of Japan's most noble and semi-historical heroes was born in an enormous peach floating down a stream. In China, peaches were consumed by immortals due to their mystic virtue of longevity (long life). Peaches are an important birthday food in Korea and Japan, especially for the 60th, 70th and beyond birthdays. Asian peaches are often more white than the western yellow peaches!

The Japanese have cultivated **Rice** for over 2000 years and it is an important part of their diet and culture. In ancient times, rice growing was a religious act and the Japanese Emperor still performs several traditional "Shinto" ceremonies to bless and protect rice crops. Koreans eat rice with every meal. It is a shorter grain rice and bland tasting to cool the heat of the often very spicy food. Half of the world's population eats rice daily. In Asia, almost every meal has rice so the calories are very important for people to have enough food to eat. Countries attach great importance to rice produced in their own country; there is a lot of pride associated with rice growing techniques. An example of the pride is —Japan and Korea both eat every bit of rice they produce and only import when they run out.

Samurai Warriors were noble class and highly skilled warriors in Japan. They were very famous for their absolute loyalty and also because they lived by a special, honorable code. They are still well-known in martial arts and will always be remembered

for their top level of "skill with the sword." Samurai warriors will come to visit Fujimini Island — how will the animals react? I'll give you a clue — Green Hamster will be dying to hold one of the swords but not everyone will be excited!

Sushi is an important food that has sticky rice, fish and sweet rice vinegar. It is typically dipped in a little soy sauce and eaten with chopsticks. Sushi usually has raw fish but can also have cooked fish, shellfish or other ingredients. It is low in fat and delicious! Sushi can be an important part of special occasion meals and recipes are often passed down in families. Sushi chefs are well trained and sushi is now one of the most recognized and popular foods originating from Asia. The Japanese are especially known for their wonderful and artistic sushi. Red Penguin is the best sushi maker on Fujimini Island.

Taekwondo is a very famous Korean self-defense martial art. At one time, the craft was considered an important military art as they needed to protect themselves from many enemies coming to their land. There is a lot of etiquette associated with the art of taekwondo and its literal interpretation is "to strike with hands and feet." A close, special relationship exists between student and teacher and the student always deeply respects his/her "sengsamneem." Globally, it is now a popular sport. Orange Bunny is the taekwondo "sengsamneem" on Fujimini Island and has awesome moves!

Drinking **Tea** is often associated with the English but tea drinking originated in Asia and has spread to every corner of the world. In Korea and Japan, elaborate tea ceremonies often feature green tea served and consumed in a traditional manner with rules of etiquette. One example is in Korea, the bride will serve her future in-laws tea on her knees, showing her humbleness and respect for the new family. Attending a tea ceremony is one of the most important and popular things to do if you ever visit Japan or Korea. Formal tea houses are also found in China, but the Chinese are more well known for their many tea houses that are packed every afternoon by students and business people.

The **Tortoise** is one of the important "protectors" in Asian culture. It is a symbol of longevity which means long life. They have a long life span and move slowly but with sturdiness and are thought to possess great strength (hard shell). They are also a symbol of wisdom. The Samurai that come to visit Fujimini Island are sea tortoises. Read about their special mission. Are they the right ones for the important task from the Emperor?

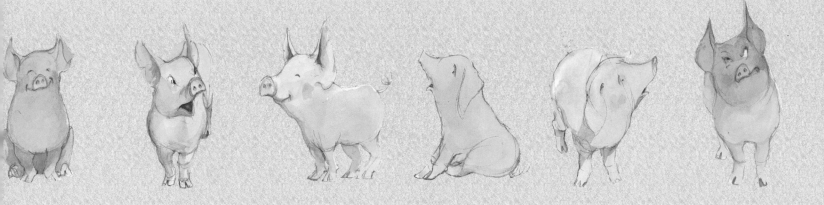

Ngox - lyn -

Keep reading a

Life -

[signature]

Pippin
the Christmas Pig

by
Jean Little

Illustrated by
Werner Zimmermann

North Winds Press
A Division of Scholastic Canada Ltd.

This story is for Maggie Jean Smart, May 14, 2002, a very special girl.
— J.L.

Dedicated to Isabella L.A. Kensington, friend & muse
— W.Z.

The paintings for this book were created in watercolour and pencil
on Arches Watercolour Paper.

The type in this book was set in 16 point Usherwood Medium.

National Library of Canada Cataloguing in Publication

Little, Jean, 1932-
Pippin the Christmas pig / Jean Little ; illustrations by Werner Zimmermann.

For children.
ISBN 0-7791-1420-5

I. Zimmermann, H. Werner (Heinz Werner), 1951- II. Title.

PS8523.I77P56 2003   jC813'.54   C2003-901063-5
                            PZ7

6 5 4   Printed and bound in Canada   04 05 06 07

Pippin stared up at Noddy, the grumpy old donkey. "Noddy, you look all excited," she said.

"Of course I'm excited," said Noddy. "It's Christmas tomorrow."

"What's Christmas?" Pippin asked.

"What's Christmas?" Noddy repeated. "Don't be pig-ignorant, Pippin. Everyone knows about Christmas."

The tips of Pippin's ears went very pink.

"I hope you remember that my family gave the first gift," Noddy went on. "The baby's mother rode on a donkey all the way to Bethlehem. Christmas couldn't even begin until she got there."

The curl went out of Pippin's tail. "Nobody told me a thing about Christmas," she said.

"*My* mother said they were almost late because of that slowpoke donkey," Bess said with a gentle moo. "My great-great-great-grandmother gave her manger for the baby's bed. Without her, they would have had to put the baby to sleep on the floor. The best present was that manger."

"What baby? What manger?" Pippin begged. Nobody noticed her. "And I still don't know what Christmas is," she said.

"The hay in that manger was full of prickles," muttered Curly. "They would have scratched the child's face. One of my family had to give the mother a lamb's fleece to cushion the rough bed. The soft wool was a welcome gift, I can tell you."

Pippin's ears were now bright pink. "But where were the *pigs*?" she demanded in her biggest voice.

"Don't fret, Pippin," Bess said. "Christmas has nothing to do with pigs. What present could a pig possibly give a baby anyway, especially a baby as special as that one?"

"If there were donkeys and cows and sheep, there must have been pigs," Pippin stated.

Once again, nobody was listening to her.

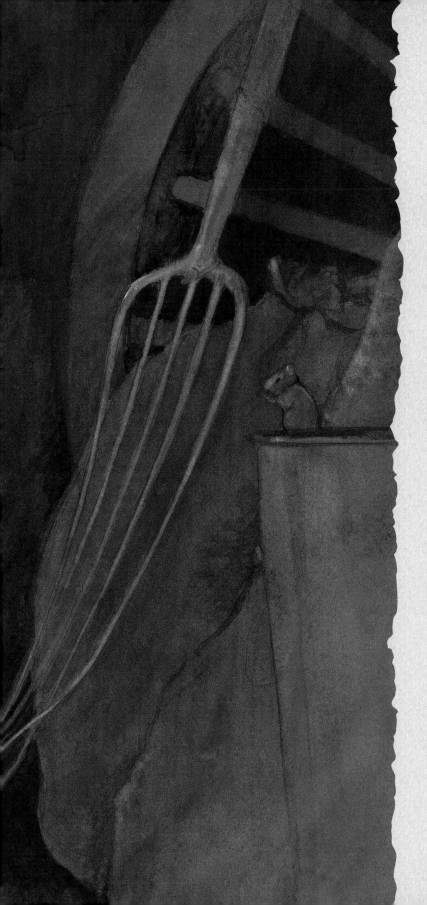

"*My* VERY-GREAT-grandparents sang him to sleep," said Coo Roo the pigeon. "That crowd of angels and shepherds kept him awake until my family crooned a lullaby. That song was of the first importance that night."

Pippin stamped her tiny hoof. "But what did the *pigs* do?" she said. "They must have been there and done something."

"No pigs were there," the others scoffed. "The very idea! The child was a king. That holy stable was no place for pigs."

Then Bess spoke up. "Pippin, face it. What could pigs have given a holy child? Pigs have nothing worthy."

Pippin hung her head. The barn door stood open a crack. Slowly, she went toward it.

Then she pushed it farther open with her snout. She had to get away.

Once outside, she waited. They might call her back.

Nobody called. They had not even noticed her leaving.

"I'm going where pigs matter but Christmas doesn't," Pippin announced in a shaking voice. "And I won't come back! Never, ever."

As she set out, a gust of
wind struck her full in the face.
Snowflakes stung her eyes and
frosted the tips of her ears. She
almost fled right back inside, but
she forced herself to go forward.

The cold was bitter. Soon
Pippin could no longer see the
barn through the whirling snow.
She passed a tattered scarecrow
who leered and waved one
ragged arm at her.

Farther on she saw a bluejay with its feathers all blown backward. The hunched bird was too miserable to warn the world of the little pig's passing.

Pippin's feet hurt and her tail stiffened into a curly icicle.

"I will die out here," she whimpered, stumbling on. "If I don't turn back, I will perish."

But she had sworn never to go back. They didn't want her. They had said pigs were good for nothing.

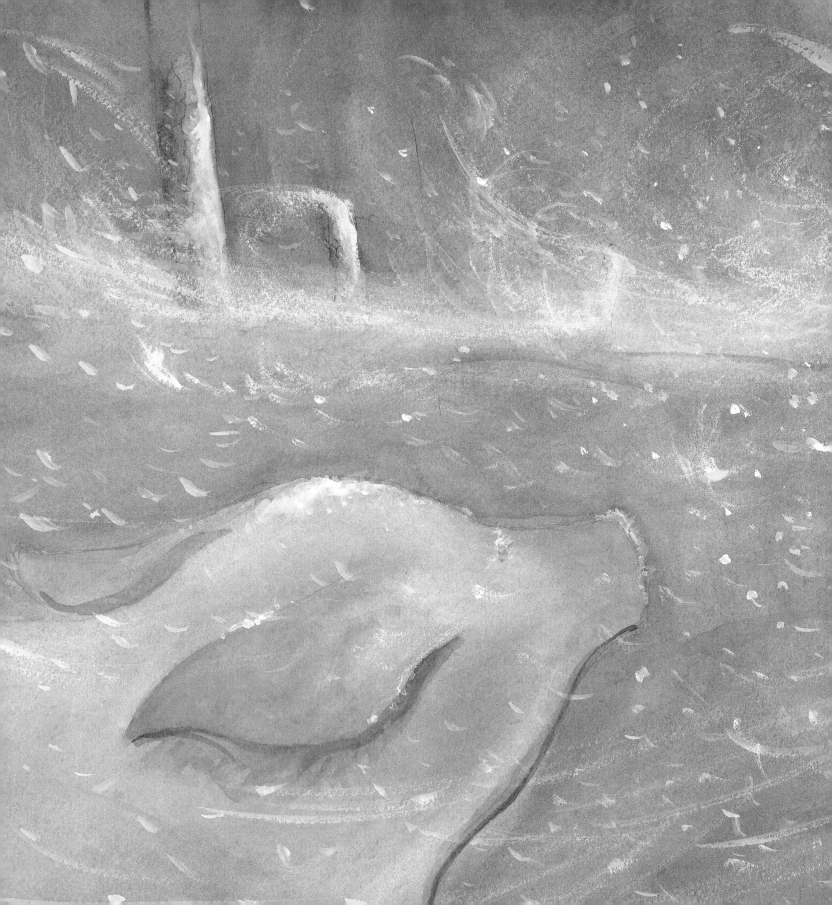

At long last, Pippin reached the main road. She peered up at the mailbox and wished she could climb inside. But she passed it and kept going.

Down the road, she stopped to catch her breath. Through the snow she glimpsed a woman coming toward her, carrying a baby in her arms.

Pippin moved closer for a better look. The woman staggered. She wore no gloves or hat, and her jacket was thin. And the little girl, so sound asleep that her head nid-nodded on her mother's shoulder, looked too heavy for her to carry much farther.

"Poor things," Pippin murmured, forgetting her own troubles for a moment.

"Shhh," the woman crooned to her baby. "We have so far to go. But maybe we can find a nice warm barn to rest in." She shivered.

Pippin knew where to find a warm barn. She had sworn never to return there, but this was an emergency. "Follow me," she grunted, and nudged the woman along the road until they came to the long farm lane.

Maybe the wind had dropped, for Pippin felt a little warmer. Even the scarecrow's smile looked friendlier.

At the barn door, the little pig pushed ahead. "Listen to me," she called to the animals.

"Don't interrupt, Pippin," said Noddy. "We're making Christmas plans."

"I don't care," Pippin yelled. "Whatever Christmas was, it was long ago. I have a baby here who needs a place to sleep *right now.*"

Bess's jaw dropped as she saw the woman clutching her baby.

"It's Christmas all over again," the woman whispered as she entered the barn. Gently she laid her baby down in the manger's sweet hay. The baby curled up and started sucking her thumb.

"Bless you, little pig. It is warm here," the woman murmured, settling onto a nearby heap of hay. "Warm and safe."

"My word, they're both asleep already," Coo Roo whispered a moment later.

Then all the animals stared
at Pippin.

"Who is this woman?" snapped
Curly.

"Pippin, we can't take in some
homeless nobody," Noddy added.

"My very-great— " Bess began.

"We'll need milk," said Pippin.
"We'll need some warm, soft wool.
We'll need your old blanket, Noddy.
We'll need lots of lullabies. Your
VERY-GREAT-grandparents aren't here.
You must help this baby yourselves."

"But that's not a special baby,"
Noddy protested.

"Of course she is," said Pippin.
"All babies are special."

Noddy gazed into the small
sleeping face. "You are right," he said.
"I'd forgotten."

When the farmer and his wife came out to feed their animals, they saw the young woman, covered with Noddy's old blanket, asleep in the hay. Then they caught sight of the baby girl lying in the manger.

"It's Christmas," the man said softly. "Right here in our barn. It's a miracle."

"Hush," his wife whispered. "Let them sleep. We'll keep watch and see if they need our help later on."

When the couple left, Pippin looked around and saw what they had seen: Noddy's warm blanket, Curly's soft wool, Bess's manger and milk.

"You were right," she said. Her tail drooped. "None of these gifts is from me. Pigs really do not have anything to give. Thank you all for being so kind to them."

The other animals looked down at the little piglet.

"Oh, Pippin, what a silly you are," Bess said softly. "You gave us our very own Christmas. You gave us a chance to give *ourselves* instead of boasting about our grandparents. Don't you see that that was the best gift of all?"

"It took a runty pig," laughed Noddy, "to teach us what Christmas is."

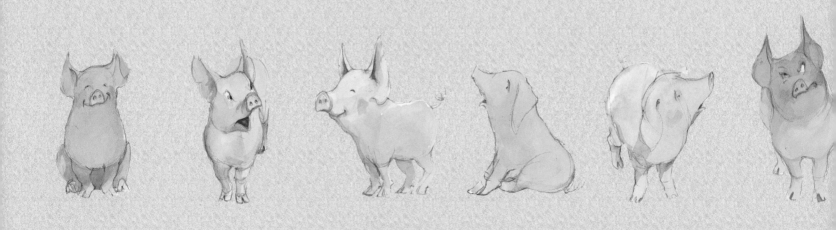